WHAT'S THAT SOUND?

by Mary Lawrence
illustrated by Lynn Adams

Kane Press, Inc.
New York

Acknowledgement: Our thanks to Marc Feldman, PhD, Physics, UC Berkeley: Professor, University of Rochester—Dearborn, for helping to make this book as accurate as possible.

Library of Congress Cataloging-in-Publication Data

Lawrence, Mary.
  What's that sound? / by Mary Lawrence ; illustrated by Lynn Adams.
    p. cm. — (Science solves it!)
Summary: Amy, Tim, and their parents go to the country, where Dad loves the peace and quiet but Tim is frightened by all the strange sounds.
        ISBN: 978-1-57565-118-7 (alk. paper)
        [1. Sound—Fiction. 2. Country life—Fiction.] I. Adams, Lynn, ill.
II. Title. III. Series.
  PZ7.L43673 Wh 2002
  [E]—dc21

2002000439

10 9 8 7 6

First published in the United States of America in 2002 by Kane Press, Inc.
Printed in U.S.A.

Science Solves It! is a registered trademark of Kane Press, Inc.

Book Design: Edward Miller

www.kanepress.com

"Here we are," said Dad. "Our home for two whole weeks!"

I looked at my brother, Tim. "Isn't this place great?"

"I think it's spooky," he whispered.

"Shhh," Dad said. "Listen. What do you hear?"

"Not much," I told him.

"Exactly," he said. "Peace and quiet at last!"

"Dad loves the country," said Mom.

"Me, too!" I said. "Come on, Tim. Let's explore."

"No way," he said. He lowered his voice. "This place looks haunted."

"Don't be silly," I said. "There's no such thing as ghosts. You know that."

"No, I don't," Tim said. But he came with me anyway—about two feet. Then he had a fit.

"Amy, what's that n-n-n-noise?" he asked.

I heard it, too—a high, squeaky sound.

"Bats!" Tim shrieked. "I'm out of here!"

We use our ears to hear. Everything we hear is sound. Sound is a kind of energy.

"Hold on," I said. I pointed up. "That squeaky sound is just baby birds crying for food."

The mother bird flew over with a worm and the cheeping stopped.

"Well, it *could* have been bats," Tim said.

During dinner that night we heard a high,
tinkling sound.

Tim's eyebrows shot up.

"That's just wind chimes," I told him.

"It's so quiet here," Dad said. "We can even
hear that tiny little sound. Isn't that great?"

Sounds can be
soft or loud.
Sounds can
have a low pitch
or a high pitch.

SOFT

LOUD

LOW

HIGH

"Why does Dad think it's so quiet here?"
Tim asked later. "I hear a million scary noises."
"Name one," I said.
"That creepy tapping noise," he whispered.
He scrunched down under the covers.

The sound was coming from the window.
I got up to investigate.

"I don't think you should go over there,
Amy," said Tim. "IT might get you!"

"Don't be a scaredy-cat," I said. I pulled back
the curtain.

"See?" I said. "It's only a moth bumping against the screen. We heard them all the time at camp last summer. Now, please go to sleep."

"But Amy. . ." Tim groaned.

It was starting to rain. "Raindrops make a nice peaceful sound," I said. "That will help you fall asleep."

After we hear the same sound a few times, we get to know what it is. Our ears and brain work together. Amy's ears heard the sound, and her brain said, "That's a moth sound."

I was dozing off when I heard a deep
rumbling noise. Thunder. The window rattled.
"Something is trying to get in!" Tim yelled.
He was halfway out of bed.

11

"That's just the window shaking," I said. "Sound waves from the thunder move through the air and make things vibrate."

"Vibrate?" asked Tim.

"Move back and forth," I said. "I had it in science. Touch your throat, like this. Now buzz— like a bee."

nerves
to brain

bones

ear canal

eardrum

tube

Sound vibrations go right into your ear! They hit your eardrum, which vibrates (just like a drum!). Then three tiny bones vibrate, too. A liquid behind the bones also vibrates. Little nerves send electrical messages to your brain—and you hear!

"Wow," said Tim. "I felt something moving."

"Vibrating," I said. "Vibrations cause sound waves. Soft sounds make little waves and loud sounds make. . ."

"BIG waves," said Tim. "That's cool."

"But I *still* say this place is full of scary noises," Tim said.

"You know what?" I said. "You make more noise than all the noises in this place put together! Can we please go to sleep?"

"Amy," Tim said. "Can I sleep next to you?"

He grabbed his blankets and made a bed on the floor before I could say a word. I said okay, anyway.

Maybe now I could get some sleep.

I was starting to have a wonderful dream when Tim grabbed my foot.

"Amy, wake up!" he whispered. "Something's moving on the stairs. It's making a creaky sound."

I didn't hear anything. "Just cover your ears and go to sleep," I said.

You can muffle sounds by covering your ears. Very loud sounds can damage your hearing. That's why some people wear **ear defenders** to block sounds. Even traffic noise and loud music can hurt your hearing—not all at once, but little by little over time.

ear defenders

Then we heard something smash downstairs. This time *I* jumped out of bed. "We'd better go see what happened," I said.

Tim shook his head.

"Okay, I'll go myself," I told him.

"Wait!" Tim said. "I'm coming."

I put my finger to my lips. Tim nodded, and we crept downstairs. A bolt of lightning flashed outside. Then came a loud crash of thunder.

Tim took my hand and held on tight. The
kitchen door was moving. . . .

Whew! There was Dad, holding a fat sandwich. "Hope I didn't scare you," he said.

"Who, us?" said Tim. We looked at each other.

"My grumbling stomach was keeping me up," Dad said. "Sorry I woke you. I dropped a plate. Are you guys hungry?"

"No, thanks," I said. "We're too tired to eat."

We went back upstairs. Tim finally fell asleep, and so did I. Even the storm couldn't keep us awake.

Dad's grumbling stomach was loud. Most other body sounds are hard to hear. A stethoscope makes them louder.

"Ah, the peace and quiet," Dad said again at breakfast.

Mom smiled.

"Tim doesn't think it's quiet here," I teased. "He thinks every little sound is a ghost."

"No, I don't," said Tim. "Last night I did, but that's because I didn't know what was making the sounds. I'm okay now—I think."

"Good," I said. "Then no more talking about haunted houses. No more worrying about ghosts or monsters. Deal?"

"Deal," said Tim.

He really meant it.

He didn't mention ghosts even once that day.

Around sunset we went out and caught fireflies. Suddenly we heard a low, moaning noise.

Wooooooooooo . . . aaaaaaaaaaaah . . . ooooooooo!

"What's that sound?" I cried. It was like nothing I'd ever heard before. I couldn't help it— I was scared.

"Let's go find out!" Tim shouted, and took off across the field.

I ran after him. "Come back!" I yelled.

The moaning seemed to be coming from an old shed. It got louder as we got closer.

Sounds get louder as we get closer to where they are coming from because the sound waves are strongest there, where they start. When we get farther away the sound waves spread out and get weaker and weaker—until we can't hear them anymore.

"Maybe we should get out of here," I said.
I really truly didn't believe in ghosts. But if
there *were* any, they'd sound like this.

"We can't," Tim said. "We made a deal.
Remember? No more ghosts."

I couldn't believe what Tim did then. He went inside.

"No, Tim!" I cried. Even though my heart was pounding, I went in after him. I had to save him from . . .

. . . a friendly old man with a tuba.

"Guess you two heard me practicing, eh?" he said. "Mrs. Hubber can't stand the noise, but I've got to get ready for the big parade tomorrow. I'm the only tuba they've got!"

"Were you scared?" Tim asked me later.

"Scared?" I said. "Of a tuba? Give me a break. What about you?"

"I wasn't scared at all," he said. "Not much, anyway."

We both started to laugh.

The next day at the parade, Tim and I waved to Mr. Hubber.

"Who's that?" Dad shouted over the music.

"Just a friendly ghost," Tim shouted back.

Mrs. Hubber was at the parade, too. She didn't seem to mind the tuba one bit. Then the wind blew back her hair, and we discovered why.

She had cotton in her ears!

I can communicate!

THINK LIKE A SCIENTIST

Amy thinks like a scientist—and so can you!

Scientists communicate. They explain to others what they are doing and learning. They may communicate by writing, drawing, or telling us what they want us to know.

Look Back

On pages 11-13, what does Amy tell Tim about the rattling window? How does she communicate? What does she do to help Tim understand?

Try This!

Get together with a friend and make matching toy kazoos.

You need:

- a cardboard tube from a roll of paper towels or bathroom tissue
- a sheet of wax paper
- a rubber band

KAZOO CODE	
Sound	**Meaning**
Long, low	No way.
Short, loud	Yes!
High, loud	Yikes!
Very soft	Maybe.

Put the wax paper over one end of the tube. Hold the wax paper in place with the rubber band. You can make different sounds by humming while you hold the kazoo up to your mouth.

Try to communicate with your kazoos. Take turns asking each other questions. Use the Kazoo Code to answer.

Now try adding to the code or making up your own.

Do you like bats?